THE NIGHT I BECAME A HERO

by A. R. Marshall

www.armarshall.com/storykeeping

STORY KEEPING SERIES

for Aricin, Talia, & Oliver
Be heroic every day. You are tomorrow's heroes.

*Note to Parents – Pick up your FREE Gifts

Thanks! You're going to love Story Keeping!

As a token of our thanks I'm offering some FREE BONUS GIFTS exclusive to my readers.

Audiobook & Parent Discussion Guide

*earbuds not included

You can download these FREE gifts at:

www.armarshall.com/storykeeping

Here's what readers are saying:

"It's fun, full of adventure, and I can't wait to read the next book!"

Samara, 9

"The story immediately pulled me in on a magnetic, compelling journey and didn't let go – dynamically weaving in surprises and subtleties. It's an absolute winner for any age."

Mike, 38

"So good it makes me speechless!"

Maddie, 7

"My kids immediately asked me to start reading the next book in the series when we finished Story Keeping, Book 1."

Rick, 36

"I loved the adventure, I hope you write a billion more books like this!"

Aricin, 8

Table of Contents

1
Grandpa's Book

Hi. My name is Riles and I am a hero. Seriously.

Not a superhero. I can't fly. I don't have super speed, x-ray vision, plastic arms, or super strength either.

In fact, I'm a pretty normal fifth grader in almost every way except one – I'm a *Story Keeper*.

Have you ever heard of a *Story Keeping*? That's okay, neither had I. It all started this summer on the first night at grandpa's house.

Ever since I can remember, Sissie, Finn and I got to spend a week of the summer at grandpa's house. Mom and dad would drop us off at the beginning of the week and pick us up seven days later. We've had so many adventures hanging out with grandpa – treasure hunts, night hikes, star-gazing, and s'mores around the backyard fire pit.

This summer grandpa took the adventures to a whole new level.

Most stories have happy endings, right? That's what makes them so much fun to read. I love rooting for happy endings. Guess what – happy endings aren't guaranteed. Some happy endings are in serious trouble. Did you know there are people that try to ruin stories – try to steal happy endings? Crazy, right?

Those stories need saving, and that's what *Story Keepers* do – they protect stories and save happy endings. I know, it sounds kind of silly, but it's true. Grandpa says people have been saving stories for centuries. His mom trained him to be a *Story Keeper* when he was a kid. She learned to protect stories from one of her great uncles. Point is, *Story Keepers* have been protecting stories for centuries!

Hard to believe? Keep reading. Let me tell you how it all started. Then maybe you'll believe me. Before *this* adventure I had no idea stories even needed protecting. But after I met Drift? Well, let's just say I'll believe almost anything these days.

I remember the night it all started. All three of us ran down the hall and slid into our beds on the triple bunk grandpa had built for us. We had a special room at grandpa's house. Across from the bunkbed, grandpa's old wooden rocker sat on a large, blue rug. Cozy under the covers, we waited – anxious and excited – for grandpa to stroll in, sit in his rocker, and tell us a story. He told us a story every night, every summer. Grandpa was the best story-teller I had ever met.

Then, we heard his footsteps coming toward the room. Grandpa walked in holding his favorite mug in one hand and a book we had never seen in the other. Grandpa always sipped tea while he told us stories. As soon as he walked in, the thick scent of Earl Grey tea filled the room. He sat down in the rocker, set his tea on the side table, and placed the book face-up in his lap.

Storytime has always been my favorite part of the day.

Grandpa hadn't turned on his usual reading lamp so the room remained dark – lit only by stars peeking through the curtains, and a slice of light from the hallway. The book on his lap looked heavy. Even in the darkness, we could see its leather sides and dusty pages. It looked strange and old.

Straining, I could see strange symbols decorating the edges and what looked like planets and a sun on the book's cover.

After he settled into his chair, Grandpa looked up.

"Children, tonight is a special night. One I have been looking forward to for some time. Tonight, I will share a special story with you – a story full of mystery, and secrets."

"And adventure?" Little Finn interrupted from the bottom bunk.

"Most definitely," Grandpa said with a smile, "With twists and turns that will put goose bumps on your arms and tickle the hair in your ears."

Sissie giggled from her middle bunk. "People have hair in their ears?"

Grandpa smiled at Sissie. "This story is more real than most stories. A story more real than a dream. Do you think you are ready?" Grandpa sounded a little serious.

"He's just trying to scare us," I said from the top bunk, "Grandpa, just turn on the light and start the story?"

"Well, alright, be patient." Grandpa chuckled, "If everyone is ready, I suppose we *could* get started. But I won't need the lamp tonight."

Then, looking down at the book he asked, "Let me see, where should we start?"

Grandpa lifted the book over his lap and let it fall open on its own. As the book fell open the pages seemed to turn themselves to a place somewhere near the middle. At the same time, something magical happened. While we watched, stretching our eyes through the starlit room, a soft white glow rose from the pages. As the glow brightened, shadows around the room grew a touch longer. The soft light glowed on grandpa's hands and reflected off his glasses.

Little Finn, Sissie and I all sat wide-eyed. We

could hardly believe what was happening. It was the first time we had ever seen a book glow by itself.

I could see a smile starting to stretch across grandpa's face as he scanned the page in silence.

Did he remember this story? Maybe he had read it once, long ago.

Suddenly, Grandpa looked up, his face lit by the book. "Shall we begin?"

2
Drift's Story

Had the pages really turned themselves? I had to ask.

"Grandpa, shouldn't we start from the beginning?"

"Not with this book, Riles," he replied. Then, he started to read.

***

Drift Elwick sat up quickly. He tried hard to open his eyes, but they felt very heavy. His head throbbed. His eyes burned. The room was too bright. All of his body ached.

Drift had the strangest feeling that he wasn't alone in the room.

Eyes closed, he tried to move his hands. They were stiff, resting at his side. He seemed to be sitting on a bed in a very bright room. Squinting, he tried to open his eyes again. His head kept pounding. He let his eyes close. He tried to relax.

Drift could hear machines humming and beeping softly on either side of the bed. Then, he heard something moving toward him. Squinting again, he thought he saw something. Was it silver? It rolled toward him. Drift's head ached. It pounded. He couldn't focus. Exhausted, he let his eyes close again. He could hear something near him.

The silver, rolling thing was very close now. It hummed, like a machine. He heard a voice – its voice – say, "Good Morning Master Drift."

The voice didn't sound human.

"Don't try to sit up. You've taken quite a fall," it said.

Something cold grabbed his arm. He felt a sharp prick.

"Ouch!"

Then, everything went black.

It was a few days before Drift woke up again. When he did, his head felt much better. He tried opening his eyes. The lights in the room must have been turned down because it felt like night. At first everything in the room looked fuzzy. After a few moments, things came into focus. Drift could see the machines, beeping and humming, dimly lit along the wall beside his bed. The room was spotless, like a hospital but more comfortable.

Slowly, Drift began to sit up. His head still hurt, but not as bad as before.

Reaching an arm behind his head, he tried to touch where it hurt – behind his left ear. His fingers found a bandage covering a nasty bump. The room was clear, but Drift's memory was still fuzzy. Where was he? How did he get here? Drift couldn't think clearly. Nothing looked or felt familiar. It was a little scary.

"That voice called me Drift. I wonder if that's my name?" he thought to himself.

Just then, Drift heard sounds outside the room. Suddenly, the metal wall across the room slid apart like an elevator door making a soft whoosh sound and in rolled a skinny robot with eyes like binoculars and wheels like a tank. The robot spotted Drift at once, and stopped.

It was clear that the robot did not expect Drift to be awake. They stared at each other for a few moments. Then, the robot spoke:

"Feeling better Master Drift?"

"I don't know, I suppose." Drift muttered, "Where am I?"

"You are in Room 17 of Bay 6 aboard Newest York – the finest space city in the Milky Way," the robot replied.

***

"What?"

I jumped up in my bunk to interrupted grandpa's story, "The Milky Way? Like the galaxy? Like our galaxy? Drift is in outer space?"

Grandpa paused and looked up from the book.

14

"That's what it sounds like to me," he said with a smile. "Would you like me to continue?"

"Absolutely!" I replied.

I could hardly believe it. I loved the thought of traveling through space. I was so excited about the book – what an adventure!

Grandpa turned back to the book, "Now, where was I...ah, yes, here we are."

***

"Room 17...blah blah blah... the Milky Way," the robot replied.

Drift watched as the robot rolled to the far side of the room and raised the shades. As he did, the most beautiful view opened up. Drift could see thousands of stars across the galaxy, and what looked like Jupiter and its moons.

"This space city must be a long way from earth," he thought to himself.

Drift tried his hardest to remember something – anything. Maybe asking more questions would help. He decided to try:

"How long have I been here?"

"It has been three months, two days, fourteen hours and thirty-six minutes since you arrived, Master Drift."

The robot rolled back toward the bed and checked the machines along the wall. Drift watched the robot carefully. He *did* remember being pricked with something sharp and he didn't want that to happen again.

In the silence, Drift's stomach growled loudly. For the first time since waking up, he felt very, very hungry. The robot turned to face Drift and asked,

"Would you like food, Master Drift?"

"Yes," Drift replied, embarrassed by the loud growl of his stomach.

The robot took a small bowl off a shelf behind Drift and placed it on a table beside the bed.

The bowl smelled delicious and Drift ate it all, quickly. Each spoonful of the smooth soup felt warm from his tongue all the way down to his belly. Each bite tasted sweet and fresh, like juicy strawberries covered in chocolate.

Drift watched as the robot continued to check the machines along the wall. After a few minutes of uncomfortable silence, he decided to ask another question:

"Do you have a name?"

"Yes," the robot replied, "My name is Alpha-Delta 42, but you usually just call me AD-42, Master Drift."

"I do?" Drift replied. The robot made him nervous.

"Yes. Do you not remember me, Master Drift?" replied AD-42.

3

First Flash

"I'm sorry," Drift said to AD-42. "I don't remember much of anything right now."

Drift felt terrible. He didn't want to hurt the robot's feelings, but Drift really didn't remember AD-42. He also didn't trust the robot – not yet anyway.

"Perhaps you need more rest, Master Drift," AD-42 replied.

"Maybe you're right," said Drift. He laid back into the bed, pulled the sheet up, and pretended to fall asleep. From under the sheet, Drift kept half an eye open to watch the robot. AD-42 finished checking the machines and rolled out of the room. The sliding metal doors closed quietly behind the robot.

Drift waited until the doors were completely closed again. Then, he sat up in bed and scanned the room. None of it looked familiar, and that made him more nervous. No matter how hard he tried, Drift couldn't shake off an uneasy feeling.

He couldn't remember anything – not his name, not the space city, not the room, and especially not that robot.

Either the bump on his head shook some memories loose, or Drift was in trouble. If only he could remember something…anything.

***

"Grandpa," Finn interrupted, "I don't trust that robot one bit."

"Me either," Sissie said from the middle bunk. "What do you think Riles?"

I didn't know what to think. Grandpa paused and looked at me, but I didn't answer.

Grandpa turned to little Finn, "Why don't *you* trust AD-42?" He asked.

"I don't know grandpa, I just don't. That robot gives me the creeps," Finn's voice grew louder as he got excited, "*Drift should not trust that robot at all.*"

Then it happened.

Right when little Finn said that last bit – that Drift should not trust the robot at all –the book flashed brighter and vibrated. The flash of light startled all of us. Sissie gave a little scream, and I jumped back in my bunk.

"What just happened?" we all whispered at grandpa.

Grandpa didn't say a word. Slowly a smile crept across his face. Then, he winked at us and got back to reading the story.

***

Wide-awake, and alone in the room, Drift decided to hunt for answers. He needed to remember something about his past before the robot came in for another visit. It was time for action. Maybe he could find a clue somewhere in the room.

Drift slid his legs out of the bed and tried to stand up – but he nearly fell. He caught himself against the bed as he tipped over. His legs were so stiff he could barely move them. Maybe he really had been sleeping for the last three months. It had seemed silly when AD-42 said it. What if the robot was telling the truth?

Looking down at his weak legs Drift noticed he was wearing strange white pajamas and no shoes. There was a number on the pajamas: seventeen.

Leaning hard against one arm, Drift tried to stand again and keep his balance – both legs wobbled. That's when he saw it.

Looking up, Drift noticed a small piece of paper slowly falling from the ceiling – like a feather. He climbed back onto the bed to reach it. Stretching up with his free hand, Drift grabbed the paper and unfolded it between his fingers.

It looked and felt like a page torn out of a small book. It had writing on it – six words:

"You should not trust that robot."

Drift's heart skipped a beat. He read the note again, slowly: "You should *not* trust the robot."

His mind began to race. Deep down, Drift felt sure the message was true. He folded the paper and quickly hid it in his pajama pocket. If AD-42 really was bad he would be back, and soon. Drift knew he had to escape, and fast.

***

Grandpa paused there and looked at each of us.

We were all still peeking over our bunks, listening to the story with wide-eyes. I'm not sure about Sissie and Finn, but I started to wonder about that message. How did it get into the room?

With a smile and a wink, Grandpa started reading again.

***

Drift scanned the room as quickly as he could – an empty desk, an empty closet, a bathroom door. He moved toward the desk on wobbling legs, pulled out the chair, and sat down to rest.

Something in this part of the room *smelled* familiar. His mind raced, trying to remember. He searched the desk frantically. All the drawers were empty.

That smell lingered. It reminded him of fresh clothes. Then, he found them – a neatly folded stack of clothes and a pair shoes that looked like his size. Drift was sure they were his. He grabbed the clothes and put them on, hiding the white pajamas in one of the desk drawers.

The smell of fresh clothes made Drift smile for the first time since waking. This new excitement gave him energy. Even his legs felt stronger. He wanted more clues. He needed to remember. Standing again, Drift searched the closet. Nothing. Next, he headed toward the bathroom. He felt sure things were going to be okay. Drift smiled.

Meanwhile, in a cold, gray room not far away, AD-42 watched Drift. Hidden video cameras showed every corner of Room 17. AD-42 watched Drift searching for clues. The robot was not smiling.

"Yes," the robot spoke into a radio, "Drift Elwick is awake. He is searching the room. We are running out of time."

4

My Hypothesis

"I knew it," said little Finn, "I knew that robot was naughty!"

Finn was right, but I wasn't thinking about the robot.

The flash of light? A falling piece of paper? Grandpa's wink? Grandpa definitely knew more than he was telling.

I had never seen a book flash and shake like that before. None of us had, except maybe grandpa. Right before the flash, Finn had shouted. Did Finn make the book flash? I wondered. What about the falling message? Was it all connected? I mean, little Finn yelled something about not trusting AD-42. Then the book flashed and Drift found the note. It all *had* to be connected, right?

Either way, this was certainly no ordinary story – and no ordinary book.

It must have been the end of a chapter because Grandpa was taking off his reading glasses and getting ready to stand up. Most nights, grandpa would only read one chapter of whatever story he picked. Sometimes, if we asked nicely, we could talk him into reading a second chapter.

All three of us must have noticed at the same time, because Sissie, Finn, and I all started begging grandpa to read more.

"Please!" we pleaded, "You can't stop there. Drift is in trouble. We have to know what happens next."

"Well, I don't know," grandpa said with a smile, "it is getting pretty late."

"Please!" we all begged again, "Pretty please!"

"Alright," Grandpa agreed, "after I refill my tea we can read another few pages."

"Yes!" I reached down to high five Sissie on the bunk below me.

Very carefully, grandpa lifted the open book from his lap – still glowing like a candle in our dark room – and set it on the side table next to his rocker.

"Now listen you three," grandpa said stepping close to our bunks, "no getting out of bed and *absolutely* no touching the book."

"Yes grandpa," we all answered. Then, he headed to the kitchen to brew another cup of Earl Grey tea. As soon as he left we all hung our heads out of the bunks to talk. Just across the room, the book sat open and glowing – inviting.

"This story is amazing!" I whispered to Sissie and Finn.

Finn agreed, but Sissie looked nervous.

"I don't know guys," she whispered, "There's something strange about this book. It feels really real, and I'm really worried about Drift."

Just then, the light from the book flickered brighter. I don't think any of us noticed it, but we should have.

"I agree." I whispered. "What do you guys think about the glowing pages? And, what about the flash of light?"

"That was awesome-sauce!" Finn blurted out in more than a whisper.

"Shhh!" Sissie and I hushed him. "We don't want grandpa to hear us talking, he might stop reading for the night."

"Oh, right." Finn whispered back in his quietest voice (which wasn't all that quiet).

I was still thinking about that torn piece of paper that fell from the ceiling in the story – the one that Drift caught and read. I had an idea about it and I wanted to test my hypothesis.

"Guys, listen up. I have an idea but I need your help," I whispered, "Why don't we try to help Drift again?"

As I spoke, the book flickered again. This time little Finn noticed.

"What was that?" little Finn loudly whispered.

"What was what?" I said.

"The book – I think it flickered," he replied.

"Really? I didn't see anything," I glanced over at the book, curious.

"It did!" Little Finn insisted.

"Riles," Sissie asked, "what do you mean we should help Drift *again*?"

"I mean," and I lowered my voice so much that Finn could barely hear from the bottom bunk, "I mean, what if Drift got the paper clue because Finn sent it to him when he told grandpa we shouldn't trust the robot?"

"Do you mean..."

"Yes," I interrupted Sissie, "I think, maybe we *can* help Drift."

Finn's eyes got really big and a smile snuck across his face.

"Riles, do you really think I helped Drift? That I sent him the clue?"

"Well, I don't know for sure," I whispered, "but I think we should..."

Just then, we heard grandpa's footsteps down the hallway.

"Quick," I whispered, and we all leaned back in our bunks.

Grandpa paused at the door to take a sip of his tea. He glanced at us kids, suspiciously. Then he walked in, careful to keep his tea from spilling.

After settling into the rocker, grandpa took another long sip of steaming tea. Then, he set the cup next to the book, and lifted the book into his lap. Before looking at the pages, he looked at us.

"Are you sure you want me to read more tonight?"

"Yes!" we all shouted.

I smiled, excited to test my hypothesis.

Grandpa placed his reading glasses just above the tip of his nose, and peered into the glowing pages. His glasses reflected the soft white light. Then, he began to read.

5

Being Watched

Searching the room, helped raise Drift's spirits. The familiar smell of his clothes was the first step toward remembering who he was, who the robot was, and why he was in space. Stepping into the bathroom, Drift saw himself for the first time since waking. He saw his own messy dark brown hair, blue eyes, and the small scar near his right eye. That scar! Immediately, Drift remembered the scar – he had gotten it saving a friend during a training mission. He recognized himself!

"That's right, I'm a Space Spy," he thought, "but why am I here? Am I on some sort of mission?"

He could remember facing dangerous robots before. Usually they didn't pretend to be his friend. What was AD-42 up to? Why pretend?

Maybe Drift had a secret – something the robot needed from him. But what? He had to remember, before it was too late.

Standing in front of the mirror, staring at his reflection, Drift noticed several blinking red lights on the walls behind him. There were four in all, spread across the open room. They looked like camera lights. He was being watched. "That robot," he thought, "AD-42 must be keeping an eye on me."

It was true, AD-42 was watching.

While Drift searched the room for more clues, AD-42 carefully tracked his every move. Catching Drift Elwick – the famous space spy – had not been easy. It had taken months. When they finally did catch him, they had to get him to their spaceship, the Mirach.

Drift was a special prisoner. AD-42 had fought in many battles trying to conquer planet Earth. Many times, they had failed. But this time would be different. This time the space pirates could not fail. They had captured Earth's legendary space spy. They had captured Drift.

It had been a long journey from their home planet in the Andromeda galaxy. The crew was restless for a new home. A new place to rule.

This time, only Space Spy Drift Elwick could stand in their way. Locked away in a prison cell, without his memory – there was no way he could defeat them.

If only they had his secret.

They had come too far to lose now. They would destroy Earth and rule the Milky Way. Victory seemed inevitable. Yet, AD-42 waited nervously in the control room. They still needed Drift's secret.

Pretending to be Drift's friend was not working. Now, the spy's memory was returning.

AD-42 had also seen that strange piece of paper float down from the ceiling. He saw Drift catch the paper, unfold it, and read it.

"What did the paper say?" The robot wondered, "And, where did it come from?" The robot watched Drift race around the room, collecting clues, remembering. AD-42 was worried.

Suddenly a loud, dark voice took over the control room speakers.

"Do you have the prisoner's secret yet?"

AD-42 was rattled. "No, Captain Kētos, we do not."

"No? Then, it is time for help. You must call *them*," the voice snarled.

"Captain, we must handle the situation ourselves. *They* are dangerous. I will get the secret myself," the robot replied.

AD-42 could see Drift rushing toward one of the cameras. The space spy got close to the lens to examine it, then took off his shoe, and smashed the camera. When he did, AD-42's video monitor went blank. One camera destroyed. All the robot could see was static. Where was Drift now? There. Across the room. The space spy ran to a second camera and shattered that lens.

"What is that sound? Is glass shattering? What's happening?" asked the dark voice.

"Nothing Captain, I have it under control," AD-42 said again.

But it wasn't nothing. As AD-42 watched, Drift destroyed the last two cameras. The robot could no longer see into Room 17.

"You do not have it under control. I do not have patience for your failure AD-42," The voice bellowed. "You must call *them*. I command you. Together, you will get what I need and bring it to me. I will not allow this space spy to defeat me again."

"Yes Captain Kētos," AD-42 replied.

The robot knew better than to disappoint the Captain.

Things were not going well. The space spy had destroyed all the cameras. Perhaps his memory was returning. If so, he really would need *their* help.

It was time to call *her*.

***

"That'll show that mean robot," Sissie smiled, "I hope Drift finds a way out."

Grandpa stopped reading and looked up from the glowing pages. Little Finn smiled wide. I could feel myself giggling inside.

"Did he get away, grandpa?" I asked.

"I don't know. Would you like me to continue reading?" grandpa replied. We all nodded, "Yes." Grandpa looked back to the book. He slid his finger across the page, "Ah yes…"

***

AD-42 could not allow Drift to escape. He slammed a button on the counter in front of him. The wall behind AD-42 slid open in a whoosh and the robot rolled quickly down the hall. Robots and alien soldiers guarded almost every door along the wide corridor. AD-42 rolled by each door as the guards saluted him.

AD-42 commanded the entire prison wing. Captain Kētos trusted him, and AD-42 could not let him down. If he failed, who knows what Captain Kētos would do – melt the robot down? Launch the robot into space? AD-42 couldn't take any chances.

No matter how dangerous she was, AD-42 had to call her. The robot needed her help. AD-42 zoomed down the corridor passing rooms on the right and left. Room 21. Room 20. Room 19. There, Room 18 – across the hall from Drift's room, the only room without guards.

Quickly, AD-42 typed a code on the wall panel and the doors slid apart with a whoosh. The robot disappeared inside.

***

"Drift's got to get out of there!" I blurted out.

"We've got to help him." Sissie and Little Finn added.

Grandpa looked up. "Help him? What would you like to do?" he asked.

"He's the good guy, grandpa," Finn laughed. "We always have to help the good guy."

Grandpa smiled.

"He's not safe in that room!" I added.

Sissie shouted, "He's got to hide!"

When Sissie yelled, the book shook and flashed. It was brighter than before and I could see grandpa smiling.

"Hey! Did you guys see that? It happened again," Little Finn shouted. "Riles, maybe you were right."

Maybe I *was* right. It all happened so fast. We needed to hear more of the story. Grandpa found his place and continued reading.

***

Drift sat down on the bed to catch his breath. He needed a plan. Just as he sat, he saw something falling from the ceiling – another piece of torn paper.

"More falling paper?" he thought to himself, "Where did *this* piece come from?"

Drift grabbed the falling message and unfolded it. This time it read:

"You've got to hide!"

Drift's eyes got bigger as he read the message a second time, then a third. He could hardly believe it. How did the paper know he was resting? Was this supposed to be another clue?

If so, Drift knew he had to hurry. Something bad must be coming. He needed a plan, and quick.

Just then the prison alarm bellowed: "Beep! Beep! Beep!"

Footsteps rushed past Drift's door in every direction.

"They must have noticed that I broke the cameras," he was scared, but the thought of a room full of robots watching him destroy the cameras made him laugh a little.

Drift quickly ran near the door and found a good place to hide. He needed a better escape plan. Maybe when the doors opened he could sneak past the enemy and get free? It would probably be his only chance.

But, who was the enemy? And, where was he – really? Could he really finish a mission without his memory? It wasn't going to be easy.

Then, with a whoosh, the metal doors slid open.

6

Two Escapes

The prison alarm blared, "Beep! Beep! Beep!"

With a whoosh, the doors to Drift's room opened and shut. Someone had slipped inside. Drift watched cautiously from his hiding place near the door. The outsider walked calmly toward the center of his room. It was a girl.

She had long black hair pulled back in a ponytail. She wore black pajamas, and no shoes. Her pajamas looked a lot like Drift's but had the number eighteen on them.

It seemed like she was looking for something – or someone. Drift stayed quiet, hidden near the door.

"Is anyone here?" she whispered, looking around the room. Drift thought her voice sounded familiar.

"Who are you?" Drift whispered from his hiding spot. She turned toward him, stared for a second, and then caught his eye.

"Oh, there you are," she replied, "Get down here. We need to leave, and quick."

"Leave?"

"Yeah, and quick. We don't have much time."

The girl ran across the room and started pushing the bed sideways.

"I don't even know who you are. How do I know I can trust you?" Drift asked.

"I'm not sure you have a choice," she replied, "If you want to stay, I guess you can sort things out with the guards."

"Guards?"

"Yeah, they'll be here any minute. Look, my name is Lark. I escaped from the room across the hall. Do you want to get away or not?"

Drift shrugged his shoulders and jumped out of his hiding spot.

"Okay, what's the plan, Lark?" he asked.

"No time to explain," she said. "Hurry over here!"

Quickly, she lifted a tile from the floor under the bed revealing a computer panel with a small slot of some kind. Lark took a card from her pajama pocket and fit it into the slot.

The panel made a soft clicking sound, and large hatch the size of nine floor tiles popped opened. A bunch of steam puffed out of the opening. Drift stared suspiciously. Did she really think he was going to jump into that hole? He wasn't sure what to think of Lark.

"What? You're not scared of a little steam, are you?"

"Well..."

"Listen, it's safe. After I learned about this secret hatch, I stole a keycard from the guard so I could escape. Before I could use the card, they moved me out of this room."

Drift was impressed. Lark smiled.

Inside the hatch was a dark hole lit by dim green lights.

"Well," Lark looked Drift in the eyes, "Are you coming with me?"

Just then, the metal doors slid open and a handful of guards rushed into the room. Aiming their weapons at Lark and Drift, they shouted, "halt prisoners, hands up."

Drift didn't need any more convincing than that. Scared or not, it was time to go.

Without a second to lose, Drift jumped feet first into the hole. Lark followed, pulling the hatch closed as she went. Screaming, they raced down what felt like a long, scary waterslide with no water and a lot of bumps.

Drift desperately tried to keep his hands up to protect his head. Every few seconds, he saw tunnels splitting off to the right and left. He could tell they were other tunnels because they had the same eerie green glow as the one they were sliding down.

Then, as quickly as the ride began, they reached the end of the tunnel Drift tumbled out of the tube and straight into a stack of empty boxes with a hard thump. They must have slid a long way. He could barely hear the alarm beeping all the way back in Room 17.

Before he could stand, Lark tumbled out of the tunnel and fell right into him.

"Sorry about that," she said. They both stood up and dusted themselves off.

"I didn't catch your name."

Drift smiled, "You never asked, and I didn't say."

As a spy, he had to be careful.

"Well," Lark said with a bit of sass, "I think I just saved your life, so you might try having a better attitude."

"You're right," Drift laughed, "I'm sorry. I've had a pretty rough day. Why don't you call me Silver?"

"Hmm," she mumbled, "Nice to meet you, Silver. Now let's get out of here."

Drift agreed. It wouldn't take long for the guards to find them. They needed to hide. Drift also needed to start remembering things. Sliding down the tube had triggered something. The dim green lights were familiar – he just didn't know why, yet. Drift glanced around the dark room. There were four tunnels led away from the room – one in each direction.

"Where are we?" Drift asked.

"Old ventilation tunnels at the heart of the spaceship," Lark explained.

"Spaceship?" Drift replied, "I thought we were on a space city – Newest York."

"Oh, is that what they told you?" Lark replied, turning to face the second tunnel, "Hardly anyone uses these anymore, and most of the guards don't even know they exist."

"Sounds like you've been here a while."

"You could say that," she said as she started walking.

Lark seemed to know her way around, so Drift followed her lead. He paid close attention to every step Lark took, memorizing the path – just in case they would have to double back. Drift had always been pretty good with directions.

The two escaped prisoners took lots of twists and turns – sometimes going left and other times going right – as they worked their way slowly upward. Their footsteps echoed in the empty, metal corridors and left prints in the dusty floor.

At first they hurried, but after a while they felt safe enough to slow down. They even felt safe enough to talk in whispers as they walked.

"So," Drift asked, "why are you being held in this spaceship?

"I should ask you the same question, Silver" Lark replied with a smirk, "If that's even your name."

Drift tried to hide his smile. He liked Lark. I mean, she had saved his life. But he still didn't know if he could trust her.

"I'm not really sure," Drift replied. "I think I got hit on the head or something. I can't remember how it happened."

"Hmm," Lark pressed, "What do you remember?"

"Not much," Drift replied, careful to not share too much.

Lark didn't ask any more questions.

A little later, as they were walking, Drift heard something – voices – echoing through the ventilation over their heads. He stopped to listen.

Lark turned to see why Drift had stopped.

"What are you doing?" she started to ask, but Drift hushed her.

He stared toward the air vent above their heads, at the top of the tunnel wall. Muffled sounds traveled down through the vent. Drift strained his ear toward the vent trying hard to hear the faint voices.

He couldn't hear all of the conversation, but he did hear something about an escape, and a girl. Were they talking about Lark? About him? Drift couldn't tell if the voices were alien guards or robots. It sounded like they needed something. Something from him? They kept saying that the prisoner had a secret – something. Was it a name? A code? It was difficult to hear the muffled voices.

"What do hear? Voices? What are they saying?" asked Lark.

"It's pretty hard to hear." Drift whispered, "Something about a code? A girl? An escape? I think they're talking about us."

"A code? What do you think that means?" Lark asked.

"I don't know," he whispered, still trying to listen.

The voices sounded really far away.

"Well?" Lark asked again.

"Shhh," Drift hushed her, "I can't hear if you're talking."

Just then, both Lark and Drift heard another sound – and this time it was much closer. Loud voices and footsteps coming toward them from both directions. Both of them froze – in less than a minute, they would be surrounded – then what? Back to the prison cell – or worse.

They had to think fast. *He* had to think fast. Drift scanned the tunnel. The voices. The vent. Drift had a plan.

"Hurry," he said, "I've got a plan. You get to follow me this time."

Drift climbed the tunnel wall and tugged at the vent cover. Pulling it loose, he tossed it to the ground. He was starting to feel like a spy again. Lark jumped out of the way as the vent cover clattered on the dusty floor sending echoes through the corridor. The voices and footsteps were just around the bend. There wasn't much time. Drift scrambled into the vent shaft and spun around quickly for Lark. He reached down for her hand.

"Now, grab on!" he cried.

Lark grabbed his hand. He tried to pull her into the vent, but it was too late. The footsteps had arrived. Guards rushed toward her yelling. Aliens and robots closed in on all sides, weapons raised. They grabbed onto Lark. They pulled her feet, drawing her back into the corridor. Screaming, she let go of Drift's hand.

"Go!" she yelled, "Go!"

So, Drift went. Quickly, he turned around and scrambled away from the guards – from Lark.

***

"No!" little Finn whimpered.

"She let go?" Sissie asked.

"That's what it says," grandpa replied.

"Keep reading," I begged.

***

The guards began yelling, "Code Red! Code Red! The prisoner escaped into upper ventilation chamber 3174. The prisoner escaped into the vent."

Drift had to move quickly. As he scrambled away he could hear the "whir" of laser weapons loading. He crawled even faster, bracing himself to dodge shots.

Over all the yelling he heard one voice yell, "Hold your fire. We need him alive." It was a robot voice – AD-42.

Drift moved quickly through the vents – turning left and right. The tiny shaft left him just enough space to crawl on his knees. He scrambled on until he felt safe. Then, exhausted, he slumped down – worn out and feeling very alone.

7
Pulled In

Grandpa finished the last sentence, and looked up at the three of us.

"Oh, grandpa, keep reading!" I pleaded.

"I think that's enough adventure for tonight," he whispered, "This story will still be waiting for us tomorrow night."

Sissie and I wanted to hear more, but grandpa could see little Finn struggling to keep his eyes open.

"Please grandpa?" I begged.

"No, not tonight, Riles."

Grandpa carefully closed the book, and set it on the side table. Standing up from his rocker, grandpa headed to our bunks and gave us each a hug and kiss goodnight. Then, he picked up his mug and headed to the door.

He stopped at the doorway. In a stern, but gentle voice he said:

"It's bedtime children. That means it's time to go to sleep. I don't want any of you getting out of bed. Do you understand?

"Yes grandpa," we all whispered.

"Good. Get a good night sleep and we can read some more tomorrow night. Remember, this story will wait for us."

We all nodded.

"And whatever you do, don't touch the book. Do you understand?"

"Yes grandpa. Goodnight. Thanks for reading. We love you," we whispered.

"I love you too – each of you," he whispered back. "Goodnight."

Then, he disappeared down the hallway.

As soon as grandpa was out of sight I leaned over the bunk to talk with Sissie.

"Isn't this book amazing?" I whispered.

I couldn't stop thinking about the story.

"Totally," Sissie whispered back, "And I think you were right. We can help Drift - two flashes and two pieces of paper."

"Isn't it crazy?" I whispered back.

Little Finn was still awake too.

"I feel sad," he whispered from the bottom bunk, "Drift is all alone. Can't we help him?"

"No, Finn, not tonight. You heard grandpa." Sissie reminded us, "He said no getting out of bed."

Sissie was always following the rules.

"Maybe we could just take a peek," I whispered.

As I spoke, the book began to vibrate softly.

"Yeah. Riles, you can read it, right? Please Sissie." Finn pleaded in a loud whisper.

"I don't know," Sissie said, "I do want to help Drift, but I think we should listen to grandpa. He said the story would wait for us. He said it twice."

The book vibrated a little more.

"Oh come on, can't we just take a peek?" I pleaded with Sissie.

Suddenly, the book flipped open, lighting the room with its soft white glow.

"Whoa," Finn whispered. "I think the book is listening to us. Maybe it wants us to help Drift too."

Then the book seemed to answer Finn. It flashed even brighter and then went back to a soft glow. I had to pinch myself – was I dreaming? Was this really happening?

We were all a little nervous – maybe even scared – but it did seem like Drift needed our help.

"Okay, just a peek," I said. "What's our plan? How can we help Drift?"

"I think he needs a friend," Finn whispered, "The story said he was feeling lonely."

The book flashed bright again.

"That's it," Sissie whispered, "We just have to read a little, and send him a note. Then, Drift will know that he's not alone."

"Okay, let's do it," I said.

We all climbed slowly out of our bunks and tiptoed across the room. Only a faint humming sound from the vibrating book interrupted the eerie silence filling our room that night. All three of us hovered nervously around the book. The pages of the book glowed beautifully, and the soft white light lit our faces.

Read a little. Send Drift a note. That was it. Easy, right?

I leaned forward looking for the place grandpa had left off. Slowly, I stretched my finger toward the book, tracking the words. Eyes wide open, we stared into the glowing book. It was beautiful.

I stretched my finger closer.

The book hummed and vibrated.

"Be careful, Riles. Remember, the story will wait," Sissie whispered.

The book vibrated more. Sissie started to get nervous.

She remembered grandpa's warning.

"Riles, don't touch the book," she shouted.

But it was too late.

I did touch the book, and the instant my finger reached the page the soft glow flashed so bright that our whole room filled with light.

I felt a sharp tug on the end of my finger. I tried to pull back, but I couldn't fight it. The tug was too strong. In an instant, the white glow wrapped around my whole body and sucked me into the book.

As I disappeared I could hear Sissie and Finn yelling: "Riles? Riles?"

I'm not sure exactly what happened next, since I had been sucked into the book. But from what I heard later, Sissie and Finn were very scared. As soon as I was gone, they tell me, the bright light dimmed to a soft glow and the book stopped vibrating.

Then, Sissie did something very brave. She leaned toward the book, careful not to touch it, and started to read.

***

A flash of white light, then darkness.

"Sissie? Finn?" Riles spoke into the cold dark.

Riles felt cool metal against his back. Too scared to move he waited for his eyes to adjust. He noticed a dim green light. He was lying in some kind of small tunnel – just big enough for crawling.

Carefully, Riles rolled to his stomach and then froze. He was face to face with a dark-haired boy. The boy looked a bit older than Riles and had a scar over his right eye.

The boy with the scar stared back.

"Drift?" Riles asked.

***

Sissie stopped reading.

"Finn, he's in the book. Riles is in the book!"

"What?" Finn replied, still scared but starting to get excited, "Riles is in the book?"

"I think so – I just read his name in the story. You heard it, right? He's in the story!"

"Whoa," Finn could hardly believe it.

Sissie moved away from the book – now less brave and more scared.

But Finn was starting to smile.

"This is kind of awesome!" Finn couldn't help imagining what it would be like to actually meet Drift.

"This is *not* awesome," Sissie shot back. "We have to get grandpa. You stay here and watch the book, and don't touch it – no matter what." Sissie warned. "Grandpa will know what to do."

Finn nodded, wide-eyed and smiling.

Sissie ran into the hall and almost toppled over grandpa. He had heard Sissie and Finn scream and was already on his way.

"What happened? Are you okay?" Grandpa asked.

"Come quick," Sissie blurted, "Riles is gone."

"Gone?"

"Gone."

Grandpa ran into the room and noticed the open book. He sat in the rocker and pulled Sissie and Finn close.

"Children, please tell me exactly what happened." Grandpa said.

Sissie and Finn took turns telling grandpa about their plan to get Drift a friend and about the book opening and flashing. They told him how

Riles had reached toward the book, and how the book seemed to swallow him up. The whole time, grandpa had a very serious look on his face, but didn't seem surprised, scared, or angry. When they were done, grandpa leaned back and thought for a moment.

"Well, this is probably all my fault," grandpa whispered to himself, "I probably shouldn't have left the book out."

Then, to Sissie and Finn, grandpa said, "I suppose we should keep reading? There's no use trying to sleep now. Would you like to hear what your brother and Drift are up too?"

"What?" little Finn asked, "So it really happened? Riles is really with Drift?"

"Well, I should hope so," grandpa replied. "Otherwise the guards will get him, and who knows what *they* would do to *Riles*."

"Oh no, grandpa," said Sissie, "Start reading right away!"

"Alright, you two hop into bed. Here we go."

Grandpa held the book up in his lap and let it fall open. Scanning the page to find his place, he began to read.

8

On Mission

Drift was confused. One moment the tunnel was empty, and then this boy appeared – out of thin air.

And the boy knew his name.

How was this possible?

"Who are you?" Drift asked.

Riles looked confused too. How had he gotten into the tunnel? Could he really be inside the story? Was the story real? Would he be able to get out? It was a lot to take in.

"I'm Riles," he replied.

"How did you get here?"

Even though Drift couldn't remember everything, he knew he was a spy, and he was pretty sure this was a secret mission. How did this kid know his name? Could he be trusted? Drift had to be careful.

"I'm not really sure," Riles replied, "A minute ago I was in our bedroom at my grandpa's house. I started to read this book – a book about you. There was a flash of white light. Now I'm here, with you – it's all kind of confusing."

***

"Drift isn't going to trust Riles," Sissie interrupted. "We need to tell Drift that Riles is a friend."

A surge of white light flickered up from the book.

"Good one Sissie," Finn laughed nervously.

"Yes, well done," said grandpa, "It seems you are getting the hang of this adventure."

He continued reading.

***

Just as Riles tried to explain the flash of white to Drift, a small piece of paper appeared out of the ceiling and floated softly toward the floor of the ventilation shaft – right between the two boys.

Drift grabbed it out of the air and read it quickly:

"Riles is a friend."

"How did you do that?" Drift stared at Riles.

"I didn't" Riles said, "at least not this time."

"What do you mean not this time?" Drift asked.

Riles smiled. He knew everything back at grandpa's house must be okay. Someone there had sent this note – Sissie, Finn, maybe grandpa. Riles felt a little more confident knowing Sissie and Finn were still with him – even if it was from outside the story.

"It's not the first clue you've received, is it?" Riles asked.

"No," said Drift. "It's not."

"Well, do you think you can trust me?" Riles asked.

Riles didn't want to explain too much to Drift, because the whole thing seemed so crazy. It was hard enough for Riles to believe it. Was he really inside a book? Who would believe that anyway?

"I think I can trust you," Drift replied. "If you know about the papers that keep falling out of nowhere, you've probably been helping me all along. So, what should we do next?"

"Well, the guards definitely saw you climb into this vent, so they will probably come looking for us. It's only a matter of time before they find us. They want you alive because they need something from you – something you can't remember, right?"

"Or something I couldn't remember," Drift smiled.

Riles smiled, "So you're remembering things now?"

"I'm starting to remember lots of stuff. I've been on this warship before. I came here for a mission."

72

"Excellent," Riles replied, "We should probably find another place to hide. And then we can make a plan. You're pretty good with directions, right?"

Drift nodded.

"Think you can get us out of these tunnels?"

"I sure do," Drift replied. "Let's go."

On they went, twisting and turning through the dim lit tunnels, heading slowly upward. Riles wanted to pinch himself – it was so much fun! He could hardly believe he was actually inside a story.

Riles had so many questions for the space spy.

"So Drift," he asked, "What do you remember about this mission?"

Drift started to explain it all as they hustled through the tunnels. Riles couldn't hear every word, because Drift kept his voice quiet and it was difficult to hear over their crawling. But the story Drift told was amazing.

"This warship – the Mirach – belongs to Kētos and his people," Drift said. "Long ago they were a band of evil space pirates stealing water from planets in the Andromeda galaxy. Then, authorities in that galaxy captured Kētos. As punishment for his evil deeds, his ship and crew were thrown out of their home galaxy forever. That's when he captained the Mirach to a new galaxy – the Milky Way."

"Wow," Riles thought, "He's from another galaxy? That's amazing."

Drift went on, "When Kētos arrived in our galaxy he was stronger than ever. He sent scouts ahead to find planets with water. One of the scouts discovered Earth. Since then, Kētos has tried to conquer Earth many times. Each time we have been able to stop him."

"So this isn't the first time you've faced Kētos?" Riles asked.

"No," Drift whispered back. "This time, he's designed a new weapon. We don't know much about it, but we fear it may destroy the planet and everyone living on it. If Kētos conquers Earth

- still the strongest planet in the galaxy – he will be able to conquer the entire Milky Way."

"We can't let that happen!" Riles whispered back.

"My mission," Drift continued, "is to stop Kētos. I need to locate the weapon, install a special computer virus we designed to disable the weapon and destroy the Mirach, and escape without being detected. Unfortunately, last time all I did was find the weapon."

"What happened?" Riles interrupted.

"Well," Drift went on, "from what I can remember, I found the weapon, but it must have been a trap. I knew I wouldn't have enough time to install the virus. Instead, I hacked into the computer and changed the pass-key. That's when, I heard someone behind me, but before I could turn around, something hit me on the head. Everything went black. I woke up with a bad headache and stiff legs. That's when I met AD-42, but I feel like you might already know that part."

"Wow, any idea who hit you?" Riles asked.

"No, but that doesn't matter now."

"It doesn't?"

"No. We have a mission to finish." Drift locked eyes with Riles, "Are you ready?"

"I think so," Riles replied nervously. It had been a long day and Riles had stepped into a bigger adventure than he ever could have imagined.

"Do you see the electrical lines running through these tunnels and vents?" Drift asked.

"Yeah."

"They lead up – toward the heart of the Mirach. That's where we'll find the weapon."

Drift knew the tunnels well, and they quickly came to an overhead hatch that opened onto the main level of the warship. He spun the hatch lock and the two boys pushed hard to lift the metal door.

Light from the main level nearly blinded them as they climbed out of the vents.

Kētos' warship – the Mirach – was bigger than a city. The outer wall of the warship looked clear like glass, revealing a 360-degree view of the Milky Way. The sun shone in brightly. It took a moment for their eyes to adjust.

Riles was amazed by the sheer huge-ness of the warship. All the space-cars and space-trucks inside the warship floated or flew. None of them had tires. Looking up Riles saw three or four layers of traffic zooming around hundreds of high-rise towers. Gigantic electronic billboards were everywhere, with pictures of Captain Kētos and his pirate army. Between the high-rise buildings and beyond the glass-like wall, Riles and Drift could see stars, planets, and moons.

Riles thought the city must be orbiting the sun somewhere between Mars and the Asteroid belt.

Space pirates on the main level seemed too busy with their own business to notice Drift and his new friend climb onto the street and duck into a nearby alley.

Drift scanned the streets trying to remember directions. They needed to get to the heart of the warship – and fast.

Riles took in the incredible view in seconds – so much to see, but no time to enjoy it. They had a mission to complete.

"This way," Drift motioned, and off he ran.

Dodging in and out of traffic, Drift and Riles ran through the space city – turning left here, then right there. They stayed mostly in the shadows and used alleys whenever possible. Drift *was* good with directions.

Then they saw it. A tall structure at the center of the main level – the heart of the warship.

9

Agent Lark

Just before Riles found himself in the vent – before Drift was alone and lonely – Lark had been captured. Drift tried to save her – tried to pull her into the vent, but when the guards grabbed her, she screamed.

She let go of Drift.

She yelled, "Go!"

Drift went.

As Drift scrambled deep into the vent, away from the trouble, the guards pulled Lark to the ground and stepped back. She stood and dusted off her clothes.

Then, AD-42 rolled forward to face her.

"Hello, Agent Lark. What did you find out?" the robot asked.

"Nothing more than you," Lark complained. "I told you to give me some time. How am I supposed to learn his secret if you don't give me any time?"

"Watch your tone, Agent Lark," AD-42 threatened.

"No, you watch your tone," Lark shot back. "I report to Master Calamitous, not to you. I came here to help you, with your problem. Your guards messed it up."

AD-42 backed down. He knew she was right. He gave orders to the other robots: "Find the space spy. Bring him to me. Alive."

Frustrated, Lark turned away and headed up the tunnel. Master Calamitous would not be happy. She needed to get the code from Drift, and fast – before the space spy remembered his mission.

"If he does remember," Lark thought to herself, "He'll head to the heart of the warship."

She knew that if Drift still had the virus, he would try to complete his mission and destroy the weapon. She could not let that happen.

Captain Kētos had to win. If his space pirates took over Earth, Drift's story would be ruined – and that was *her* mission. Ruining stories makes Master Calamitous very happy.

"Drift will still think I am his friend," she thought to herself, "It's time to end this."

In a dark red flash, she disappeared from the tunnel completely.

***

"Wait, what? Lark's bad?" Sissie asked, "Where did she go?"

"Oh no," yelled Finn, "We've got to warn Riles and Drift about Lark – *She's dangerous!*"

Again, the book gave off a bright white flash. Grandpa looked concerned – maybe for the first time. He hadn't expected this twist. He didn't take his eyes of the page. He just kept reading.

***

Drift and Riles raced through space traffic – steadily closing in on the heart of the warship. The building that held Captain Kētos' weapon loomed over them, less than a block away.

Running hard, moving in and out of shadows, they finally arrived at the large columns surrounding the entrance to the heart of the warship. Slipping stealthily between columns, they reached the large front stairs and raced toward the door.

That's when they noticed a small piece of paper falling in front of them.

Neither boy saw the flash of dark red light behind them.

Riles grabbed the paper out of the air.

"So there you are! I'm glad to see you got away," a voice called out from behind.

Drift recognized the voice – it was Lark.

Both boys turned to face her.

Drift stepped toward Lark - excited to see her alive.

"How did you escape?" he asked.

"Who's he?" Lark asked, ignoring Drift's question and looking at Riles with a stale expression.

"Never mind that, it's a long story," Drift replied. "My memory is coming back and we need to hurry."

Lark didn't move. She continued to stare at Riles.

"Are you sure he's a friend?"

"Yes, I'm sure," Drift replied, "Now let's get going. We need to get inside, and quick! Finally, I can complete this whole messy mission."

"Do you remember the code?" she asked.

"Huh?" Drift replied.

"The code. Do you remember it?" Lark repeated dryly, shifting her eyes to Drift.

"How do you know about the code?" Drift replied.

He didn't remember telling her about any code.

Suddenly, he remembered why her voice was familiar. He had heard it before – right before everything went black. His jaw stiffened as he locked eyes with Lark. She had never been his friend.

"Do you remember it?" Lark repeated, growing impatient.

Riles remembered the clue in his hand. Slowly, he tried to unfold it in his hand so he could read it.

Lark grabbed his arm.

"Give me the paper." She said, shifting her gaze back to Riles.

"Lark, what are you doing?" Drift stepped closer. "It's been you all along – hasn't it. Who are you, really?"

Ignoring Drift, Lark tightened her grip on Riles' arm.

"Give it to me." She repeated.

Riles slowly turned over his hand and opened it. Lark snatched the paper from his hand and shoved him to the ground.

"Well," Drift stepped closer, "What does it say?"

She laughed, and held the paper out for both boys to read:

"She's dangerous!"

"Guess you got this one a little too late, eh boys?" Lark smiled an awful, mean smile.

As she spoke, guards stepped out from hiding places all around the building.

It was all a trap. Lark had caught them.

A whole army of guards had them surrounded. There must have been a hundred laser blasters pointed directly at Drift and Riles. There was nowhere to run.

"Who are you?" Drift looked at Lark with hard eyes.

"I'm Lark. Agent Lark," she replied.

Turning to Riles she added, "You must be the boy I keep hearing about. You have a sister and brother too, right?"

Riles didn't say a word. How could she know that?

"Hmm," she laughed at him. "Not as impressive as I had expected."

AD-42 rolled up, facing the boys.

"What now, Agent Lark?" the robot asked.

"Lock them up, of course," she replied. "And get me that code!"

Then, in a dark red flash, she disappeared.

10

Sissie's Plan

This was not the ending grandpa had imagined. "How could I let this happen?" Grandpa wondered aloud, "Riles needed more training. Now, it's up to the rest of us to save him."

Sissie and little Finn were worried too. It seemed like Lark was winning. How was Drift going to shut down the weapon from his prison cell? Would Riles ever get out of the book?

Then, Sissie had an idea – an incredible idea.

"Grandpa," she whispered, "we can send them clues, right?"

"It seems like we can, sweetie," he whispered back.

"And Lark knows what the clues are about, right?"

"Well, it seems like she knows at least something about the clues."

"And it seems like Lark can flash in and out of the story, right?" Sissie asked.

"Yes," grandpa smiled.

"Do you think Lark is like Riles?" she asked.

"Maybe," grandpa replied.

"Wait a minute," Finn chimed in, "Do you think she got sucked into the book too?"

"Perhaps," grandpa replied, and then under his breath he muttered, "But how did they find *this* story?"

"What's that grandpa?" Sissie asked.

"Oh, nothing sweetie," grandpa flashed a fresh smile at Sissie and Finn.

Maybe they could save Riles after all.

"Anyway," Sissie went on, "I think Lark might be able to move in and out of the book whenever she wants."

"Whoa," said Finn, "that would be crazy awesome!"

"Yeah," Sissie laughed. She was starting to get excited, "And if Lark can jump around in the story, maybe Riles can jump around too – he just doesn't know it yet."

Grandpa, Sissie, and Finn started working on a plan to rescue the boys. Drift and Riles would have to get free, finish the mission, and get home safe. It wouldn't be easy – but their plan might just work.

When Sissie, Finn, and grandpa finished planning, they turned back to the book and continued reading.

***

After Lark vanished, AD-42 ordered the guards to lock both boys in electromagnetic handcuffs and shoved them into the back of a hover van. Drift and Riles sat next to each other, facing two guards. AD-42 had ordered them back to the prison cells, and the guards were taking no chances this time.

"Did you see Lark disappear into thin air?" Drift whispered to Riles.

Riles nodded. He was wondering about Lark. She had given him a strange look when they met. She seemed to know about him – and about Sissie and Finn too.

Something wasn't right.

Riles had also noticed Lark disappear into thin air. And the dark red flash she made reminded him of the white flash grandpa's book had made.

Just then, a small piece of paper started falling from the ceiling of the van. Then another. Then another. What started as one piece quickly became five, then ten, then fifty, then hundreds. In just a few seconds, papers covered the floor of the hover van.

The guards started to panic. One radioed the driver:

"Pull over. The back is filling up with papers."

"Papers?" replied the driver. "We can't pull over. We are under strict orders. No stops until the prison."

Drift watched in shock. He could hardly believe what was happening. Riles watched with a smile. He knew Sissie and Finn were up to something. He just had to figure out what they were trying to tell him. A few seconds later, their feet were covered by papers. Then their ankles, then their knees. The papers didn't stop.

"Pull over *now*. This is an emergency," the guard radioed again from the back of the van. "We can hardly see the prisoners. There are too many pieces of paper falling."

Riles knew they were running out of time. He could hear the guard on the radio.

"Pull over," the guard sounded afraid. "We're buried chest deep in paper and it's not stopping!"

Then, the van stopped. He could hear the driver hurrying to the back of the van. In a moment, the doors would be open. He had to try something – and quick. He grabbed Drift's arm.

The back of the hover van swung open. The guard looked inside just in time to see a bright white flash of light as thousands (maybe millions) of small bits of papers poured into the street. Inside the van, two guards frantically dug through the piles of paper looking for the prisoners, but all they found were two pairs of electromagnetic handcuffs, still locked.

The prisoners had escaped. The driver radioed AD-42 with the bad news.

"Sir," he said into the radio, "the prisoners are missing."

"What?" AD-42 yelled into the radio. "How did this happen?"

"We don't know," the driver replied. "The van is full of torn paper and the prisoners are missing."

There was a long pause on the radio. Then, AD-42 asked, "What's written on the paper?"

"What?" The guard replied.

"The paper – what does it say?" repeated AD-42.

"They all say the same thing," the driver replied.

"WHAT DOES IT SAY?" AD-42 yelled into the radio.

"Just five words: 'You can move like Lark.'"

***

"It's working!" Sissie squealed, "It's working!"

Little Finn gave Sissie a high five. Grandpa continued to read.

***

For Drift and Riles, darkness followed the white flash – darkness and cold. Then, as their eyes adjusted, the boys recognized the dim green lights of the warship's vent system.

It worked.

A huge smile crept over Riles' face.

"That was amazing," Riles whispered to himself.

"What just happened?" Drift asked.

"I'm not really sure, but I think I can move around like Lark." Riles replied with fresh confidence. "Are you ready to shut down that weapon?"

"You bet," Drift replied, "Let's do this!"

11

Captain Kētos

Sissie and little Finn could hardly contain their excitement, giggling with each sentence that grandpa read.

"They're doing it, they're doing it!" Finn shouted.

Grandpa continued reading.

***

Riles grabbed ahold of Drift's arm again.

In another white flash, Riles and the space spy vanished from the vent. With a flash of light, they reappeared in front of the broad doors where they had met Lark. This time, the entrance was deserted. They ran up the stairs and through the doorway. Drift led Riles across the open hall and into the elevator.

Drift hit the button for the basement.

"The guards must still be near the van," Riles thought to himself.

The elevator dropped to the building's lowest level and the doors slid open with a "whoosh."

Drift raced out of the elevator and headed straight for the computer that controlled Kētos' weapon. Riles followed. Finally, Drift could finish the mission: stop Captain Kētos and save Earth.

For the first time in a long time, Drift thought they might see a happy ending.

Riles scanned the room for danger.

Drift located the weapon. Quickly, he removed a large metal panel which hid the computer and keypad. Drift slid out the keyboard and began to type – hacking into the weapon.

Riles kept scanning the room. He noticed blinking cameras mounted on nearly every wall. Riles knew guards would arrive any minute. If only Drift could work a little faster. Would they finish in time?

Behind the cameras, AD-42 watched. As soon as he saw Drift and Riles enter the building, he notified the guards. When the boys entered the bottom level, he called Captain Kētos himself.

The situation was dire. AD-42 had to stop the space spy.

While Drift typed, guards ran up the front steps into the building, just a few floors overhead. Soon they would be in the basement. Soon this would all be over.

Drift continued typing.

"I'm in," he whispered to Riles.

"In?"

"Yeah, inside the computer system. I hacked it."

"Great!" Riles let out a sigh of relief, "What now?"

"Now, I just need to download the virus," Drift whispered.

Drift kept typing. He didn't have the virus written down anywhere – the whole thing was in his head. That was his secret. He began typing the computer virus from memory.

Riles could hear footsteps coming down all fours staircases.

"Hurry!" Riles whispered.

He could see the light on the elevator – each blink bringing guards one floor closer.

"Hurry!" Riles whispered again.

Already, it seemed too late. Guards were rushing into the room from each staircase, blasters in hand, lining up along the outer wall.

Then, the elevator stopped at the bottom floor. With a whoosh, the doors slid open. Out rolled AD-42, leading the way.

Behind the robot, a dark, towering figure stepped from the elevator and walked slowly toward the boys. He wore an evil smile.

Riles recognized the dark figure. The same face decorated electronic billboards all over the warship – it was Captain Kētos himself.

Drift and Riles were completely surrounded.

"So, space spy," came the dark, angry voice of Captain Kētos, "we meet at last."

AD-42 rolled out of the way as the infamous space pirate – the captain of the Mirach – glided toward them. Captain Kētos closed the gap between the elevator and the boys in just a few long strides. Towering over them, he filled the room with fear. The guards began stomping their feet – "Stomp, stomp, stomp" – a wicked cheer for their space pirate captain.

The whole mission seemed lost. How could this happen? They had come so far.

Then, Drift shouted, "It's done!"

He had been so busy typing that he didn't notice the guards or Captain Kētos. Turning away from the computer, Drift saw the pirates, AD-42, and Kētos for the first time.

"Whoa. Now what?" Drift whispered, standing next to Riles.

"Now," said the evil Captain, "I win."

Just as he spoke, the warship began to shake. Drift looked at Riles with a bit of surprise and hope.

"Mission accomplished?" he smiled.

"What's happening to my ship?" Captain Kētos bellowed.

AD-42 shoved the boys aside and rolled straight to the weapon. Grabbing the keypad, the robot began typing frantically.

"It appears Agent Drift has infected the weapon," AD-42 looked toward Captain Kētos.

"WELL, FIX IT!" the evil space pirate screamed.

"Captain, there is nothing I can do," the robot reported, "The weapon is already overheating. The whole ship will be destroyed."

As the ship shook, the guards panicked. Most lowered their blasters and ran every which way looking for a quick escape. No one cared about Drift and Riles if the whole ship was about to blow! It was every pirate for himself, now.

The whole building shook. The weapon glowed red-hot.

"We've got to get out of here!" Drift shouted. "Riles, now!"

Riles grabbed ahold of Drift and wished away. Just like in the van, the boys felt a white flash pull them.

"NO!" Captain Kētos yelled, lunging toward the boys.

As they disappeared from the room, they could see Kētos diving at them. They had escaped. Drift and Riles reappeared just outside the heart of the warship. The weapon began to explode.

Riles turned to Drift, "That was amazing!"

"I know," Drift said, "but it's not over yet. We have to get off this warship before it explodes."

The main level of the Mirach shook violently, tossing the boys off their feet. Guards and robots ran in every direction – hurrying to escape the exploding warship. Overhead, vehicles collided into space-scraping towers, and electronic billboards came crashing to the main level in explosions of fire.

"Follow me!" Drift shouted, jumping to his feet and pulling Riles up. "I have a space pod hidden for my escape. It will fit both of us!"

Both boys began to run. Then, a dark red flash distracted them. Lark was back.

"Where are you two going in such a hurry?" She called at them.

Lark was still trying to win.

Still trying to ruin a happy ending.

12
Agent Riles

"DRIFT, RUN!" Riles yelled.

"I'm not leaving you behind," Drift shouted back.

"JUST RUN, I'll be fine" Riles yelled, and he turned back to face Lark.

Drift didn't want to leave, but he trusted Riles. He ran as hard as he could for the space pod. He wondered if Riles would make it before the whole ship exploded into outer space.

At the heart of the warship, with explosions in the air and the ground shaking, Lark and Riles faced off. The rivals stood just a few feet from each other.

"So, you're starting to figure things out, huh?" Lark taunted him. "Well, this is my story, and I'm not letting you stand in my way."

"What are you talking about?" Riles shouted back.

He was still confused – who was this girl, and why did she want to destroy Drift?

Lark disappeared in a dark flash. Riles spun around to look for Drift. Several blocks ahead Riles saw another dark red flash. Lark reappeared next to the space spy.

Instantly, Riles wished himself there – to that exact spot on the spaceship. He could see it. In a whirling flash, he reappeared there – standing right between Lark and Drift.

"DRIFT, RUN!" he shouted again.

This time, before Lark could disappear, Riles lunged at her and grabbed her arm.

Drift ran hard, not daring to look back. The whole ship was about to blow. He had to get to his space pod!

Behind him, Lark wrestled Riles. She struggled to break his grip. He had to hold on. His hands began to slip.

Riles did the only thing he could think of – he wished himself home. Suddenly, in a swirling tornado flashing dark red and bright white, Lark and Riles spun into the air. Then, in a blink, they vanished.

***

"What? Where did they go?" little Finn shouted.

Just then, the book started to vibrate and a swirling white light shot out of the book. I fell to the floor in the bedroom.

"Riles, you're back!" Sissie wrapped me in huge hug, and little Finn joined in.

"Welcome home Riles," Grandpa said.

"Thanks guys!" I sighed. I was exhausted.

"What about Drift, did he make it to his space pod? Did he escape the explosion?" I asked anxiously, looking to grandpa for answers.

"I don't know. Let's find out," Grandpa replied.

We all crowded around the book.

Looking over grandpa's arm I saw the only words left on the page:

"Drift completed his mission. The space pirates were defeated, and the people of Earth lived to see another day."

After grandpa read those words, the soft white glow on the pages faded. Grandpa closed the book and turned toward us kids.

"But what happened? How did he do it?" I asked.

I had so many questions!

"I'm not sure we get to find out," grandpa answered softly.

"I don't understand," Little Finn replied, "Where's the rest of the story?"

"Are those really the last words?" Sissie asked. "You were in the middle of the book."

"It is confusing, isn't it Sissie," grandpa replied. "But magical books are full of secrets. I know one secret we learned tonight..."

"What's that grandpa," Little Finn asked.

"Why, we learned that happy endings can be saved didn't we," grandpa replied with a smile. "Well done *Agent Riles*."

"*Agent* Riles?" I asked.

"Yes," grandpa smiled, "*Agent* Riles. You earned that honor saving Drift's happy ending. Well done."

"Alright! Way to go, *Agent Riles*," Sissie and little Finn cheered.

"Three cheers for all of us!" I laughed. "We all saved the happy ending. There's no way I could have done it without the rest of you!"

Sissie and little Finn beamed. What an adventure!

"Alright, everyone to bed – for real this time," said grandpa.

"Seriously?" I said, "After that crazy adventure? You can't expect us to fall asleep tonight!"

"It certainly was a crazy adventure," grandpa replied. "But now it's time for bed. You'll drift to sleep quicker than you can imagine. Adventures like tonight's are exhausting – trust me. And this time, I'm taking the book with me."

Grandpa tucked us all back into our bunks, gave us hugs and kisses goodnight, and headed to the door. This time he held the book tight.

"Do I need to remind you to stay in bed this time?" he asked.

"No grandpa," we all smiled. "That's enough adventure for one night.

"Get some sleep. There's no telling what new adventure is waiting for us tomorrow."

And with a wink, grandpa left the room.

I got the feeling grandpa knew exactly what adventure was waiting for tomorrow.

Part of me wanted to stay up all night talking with Sissie and Finn about Drift and Lark and the space pirates, but grandpa was right – I felt really tired.

We all agreed to go to sleep. We would talk about the adventure in the morning.

I slept well that night – so well that I would have slept through breakfast if Finn hadn't crawled into my bunk with a million questions. I tried to bury my head under the pillow, but he just kept asking:

"What was it like to jump around in white flashes?"

"Was it cool when the hover van filled up with paper?"

"Was AD-42 scary? What about Captain Kētos? I bet he was super scary, right?"

"What was it like to be in space?"

I gave up trying to sleep and started answering little Finn's questions.

Now that the adventure was over, I had some questions of my own. Maybe grandpa would have some answers.

When Sissie woke up she jumped into my bunk too. All three of us kept talking about everything that had happened. We were pretty proud of our adventure.

I'll never forget that first mission – the first-time grandpa trained us to be *Story Keepers*. So much has changed since then. I'm not sure any of us knew quite what we were getting into – how could we? Even grandpa learned a thing or two that night.

That night was the start of something really special. Still today, Sissie, Finn, and I do our best to fight for the good guys. Even the strongest heroes need help sometimes.

Really, that's what it means to be a *Story Keeper* – helping heroes when they need it, protecting happy endings.

Storytime is still my favorite part of the day. And we still jump in and out of stories most nights. We've learned a lot since that first story, like how Lark knew about me, and what my parents were really doing that summer.

We also learned that you can't jump into any story, and you can't always help people the way you want. It's nice that Sissie, Finn, and I have each other – and grandpa. We're all learning how to protect happy endings together.

And grandpa's a really good teacher. He says we have to figure most of it out on our own – like he did when he trained to be a *Story Keeper* – but he's always there to support us when we need advice or another set of hands.

So, that's how it all started for me – a normal summer for a normal kid.

A normal kid who gets to be a hero.

Book 2 (*sneak peek*)
from The Night We Met A Dragon

1
Dragon Cover

"Hurry up - It's 7:58!" Sissie hollered from her middle bunk.

"We're going as fast as we can!" I shouted back, spraying toothpaste foam all over the sink and bathroom mirror.

I glanced at Finn, who brushed his teeth frantically, next to me. Drool covered his face. We only had two more minutes. No way was I missing story time tonight - Showers, check, pajamas, check, clean room, check, teeth brushed - working on it!

It had been three nights since our first story keeping adventure with grandpa and we couldn't wait for another chance to dive in to a magical story! For two straight days Sissie, Finn, and I had talked about our adventure with Drift. We were all anxious for another story to "keep," and grandpa kept hinting that he had more books that needed "keeping."

We had hoped to start another book the very next night, but grandpa had some friends over for dessert. Everyone left way after bedtime, so we didn't have a chance to read. Last night we stayed up too late playing games.

Tonight, grandpa said we had to be ready for bed by eight o'clock or we wouldn't have enough time to read the bedtime story.

We had to be ready by eight.

I grabbed a small towel to wipe my face and Finn's. Then, the two of use rushed into our bunks as Sissie yelled for grandpa:

"We're ready!"

Grandpa didn't say a word, but we could hear his footsteps coming down the hall. My heart pounded out of my chest - all that racing around to finish chores - but we made it.

Pausing at the door, grandpa smiled. I think he liked story time almost as much as we did. Especially with these books. A few nights ago, when he read about Space Spy Drift Elwick, grandpa did a lot of winking and smiling. I'm pretty sure he was having as much fun as us kids. Now, he stood in the doorway holding his cup of tea – and a new book.

Sissie and Finn noticed it too:

"Whoa grandpa!" Finn blurted out in a loud whisper, "Cool book."

The dark-green cover looked dusty and old, like Drift's story. Grandpa walked toward the bunk, holding the book at his side.

"Children," grandpa spoke softly, "This book has been in our family for many generations. It's been one of *my* favorite adventures for many years - since I attended grade school. In fact, my grandmother first read it with me when I was about your age, Riles."

"Really?" I asked in a whisper.

"Have mom and dad ever read this book?" whispered Finn, looking at the dragon on the cover.

"They have," grandpa replied in a distant voice, "yes. They have."

"Can we?" Sissie followed.

"Yes, of course sweetheart," grandpa replied, "That's why I brought it up tonight."

"What's it about grandpa?" Finn asked from the bottom bunk.

Grandpa smiled, "I don't want to spoil the fun, but I will tell you it's got everything a good story needs - a villain, a hero, and a few surprises. Would you like a closer look?"

"Yes," all three of us blurted out, excited for another incredible adventure.

Grandpa held out the book so that each of us could see the cover. It was beautiful. A strange creature filled the cover, zig-zagging its scaly body across the leather binding. It had detailed scales and two large wings. The book looked old, but up close you could hear it humming - like it was alive. I couldn't tell for sure in the dim light of the room, but the creature on the cover seemed to move - ever so slightly - as grandpa held out the book.

Tucking it back under his arm, grandpa walked the book to his rocking chair. He placed a steaming cup of tea on the side table, sat in his rocker, and positioned the dark-green book in his lap.

"Shall we begin?" grandpa asked.

"Absolutely!" we all answered.

Each of us kids nearly burst with excitement. After two full days of waiting, the next adventure was finally opening up!

Grandpa balanced the book upright, on its binding, in the middle of his lap. Maybe my eyes were playing tricks on me, but the creature on the cover definitely looked like it was moving - slithering back and forth on the cover. Even though the book was still closed, the pages began to glow with a soft white light.

As grandpa pulled his hands away, the book fell open in his lap. The pages shuffled themselves left and right. We all watched, wide-eyed with surprise. Grandpa paid little attention to the magical book. He took a sip of tea as it shuffled back and forth. He set his mug back, pulled reading glasses from a shirt pocket, and set them on his nose. Soft white light from the book reflected off his glasses. Grandpa looked at the shuffling pages.

"Alright, where do you want us to start reading this time?"

"How about the beginning?" I laughed.

"I wasn't asking you, Riles, I was asking the book," Grandpa smiled.

The pages slowed, then another page turn, then the soft glow pulsed.

We all sat on the edge of our bunks - speechless at the wonder of this magical book.

"Isn't that interesting," grandpa muttered.

Then, he began to read...

Ready for more Story Keeping?

I know what you're thinking: "It can't end there!"

Don't worry, it doesn't.

Find out what happens next...

✓ Will our Story Keeping heroes jump into another book?

✓ Will they meet Agent Lark again?

✓ What about Master Calamitous? Is he still trying to ruin happy endings?

✓ Does Grandpa know more than he is telling?

✓ And, where did their parents really go that summer?

Two Requests:

1. Would you be willing to leave a review on Amazon? It'd be a **huge** help – Thanks!

2. Snag your FREE GIFTS at www.armarshall.com/storykeeping

Made in the USA
Coppell, TX
20 December 2019